The Wind *in the* Willows

Kenneth Grahame
Adapted by Lesley Sims

Illustrated by
Mauro Evangelista

Reading Consultant: Alison Kelly
Roehampton University

Contents

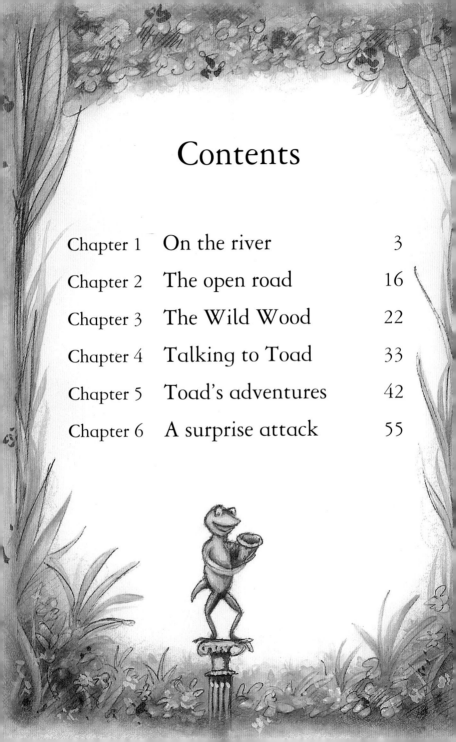

Chapter 1

On the river

Mole had been cleaning all morning and he had had enough.

"Bother!" he cried at last, flinging down his brush and heading for his tunnel to the outside world.

He scratched and he scrabbled
and he scraped with his paws, until
POP! he was out in the sun.

"This beats spring-cleaning!" Mole
cried, dancing around a hedge.

4

As he wandered along, he came across a river. Mole had never in his life seen a river before.

It chuckled and gurgled, rippling with glints and gleams and sparkles. Mole was bewitched.

He was gazing at the river, when a small brown creature appeared on the opposite bank. Then it winked – it was the Water Rat.

Mole and Rat looked at each other for a moment.

"Would you like to come over?" called Rat.

"It's all very well to *talk*," Mole grumbled. "But I can't swim."

Rat stepped into a small boat and rowed across to Mole. "Jump in!" he said, with a grin.

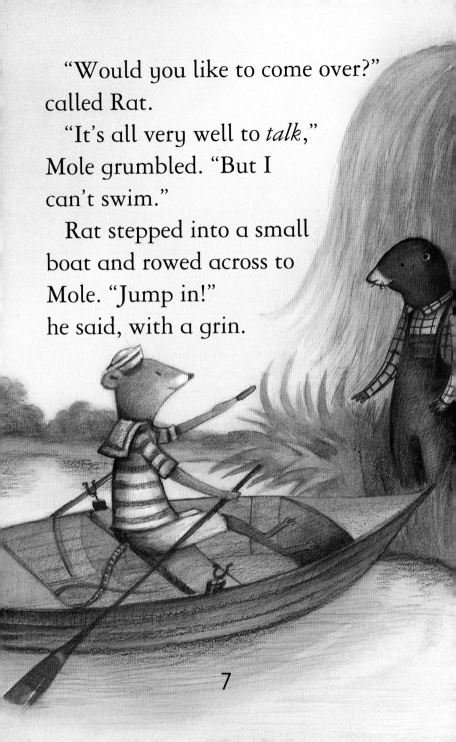

Mole took Rat's paw and carefully climbed aboard. He smiled in astonishment. "I've never been in a boat before."

"What?" cried Rat. "Never? What have you been doing then?"

"Is it as nice as all that?"
asked Mole, shyly.

"*Nice?*" said Rat.
"There's simply
nothing better..."
He drifted off
into a dream and
crunch!

The boat struck the bank.
"Oops!" Rat said, laughing,
and pulled away down the river.

Mole sat back, trailing a paw in the water and enjoying the gentle sway of the boat.

"What's over there?" he asked, sitting up and pointing to some trees in the distance.

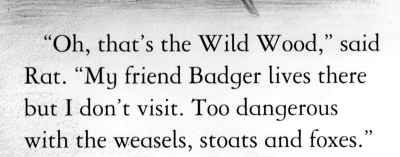

"Oh, that's the Wild Wood," said Rat. "My friend Badger lives there but I don't visit. Too dangerous with the weasels, stoats and foxes."

Before Rat could say more,
Mole spotted a stream of
bubbles and Otter's
wet, brown head
popped up.

"Everyone's on the river
today," he gasped. "I've just
seen Mr. Toad in his new boat
– new outfit, new gear, new
everything! Can't stop." And,
with a splash, Otter was gone.

11

Rat frowned. "Typical," he said. "Toad's a great fellow, but he always wants something new. Then, as soon as he has it, he's bored."

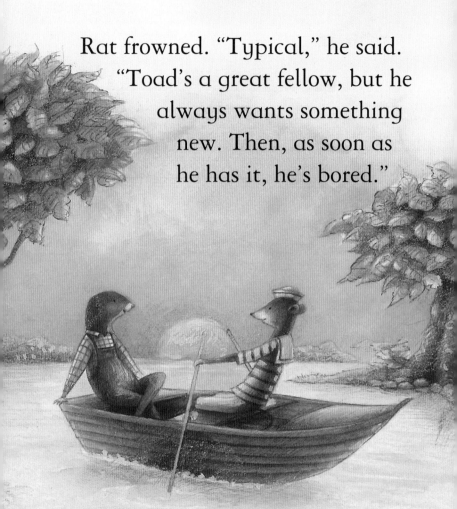

They stayed on the river until the sun sank in the sky. Mole watched Rat pulling the oars and decided he wanted to row.

Excited, he
jumped up and
snatched the oars.

Then he
plunged them
into the water...

slipped, flew
into the air...

and landed
oomph! on Rat.

In a panic, Mole grabbed at the side of the boat. Sploosh! The boat went over and he was in the river – a very cold, wet river.

Coughing and spluttering, Mole was going under when a firm paw reached out to haul him to safety.

"Oh Ratty," he sobbed, a soggy lump of misery. "I am so s-s-sorry." Rat smiled. "Don't think any more about it. But how would you like to stay with me for a while? I could teach you to swim and row."

Mole was so pleased, he could only nod as they squelched home.

15

Chapter 2

The open road

One bright summer morning, Rat was writing a poem about ducks when Mole appeared.

"Ratty," he said, "can we visit Mr. Toad?"

"Of course!" cried Rat, jumping up. "We'll row there at once. It's never the wrong time to visit Toad."

Mole gasped as he saw Toad Hall – a grand house with a lawn that went right down to the river.

17

Toad was in his garden, studying
a map. "Hooray!" he said, as Rat
and Mole strolled up. "You're just
in time for a trip in
my new caravan."

"I thought you had a new boat?"
said Rat.

"Oh pooh!" said Toad, rudely.
"Boats are boring. Wait until you
see my wonderful caravan."

There was no doubt it had everything they might need for a few days away, and all so cleverly stored. Soon, they were on the open road. Even Rat, who missed his river, enjoyed ambling along the narrow lanes.

He and Mole were walking
beside the caravan, talking of this
and that, when Poop! Poop! A car
swept past, throwing up a cloud
of dust and knocking the
caravan over.

Rat jumped up and down in fury,
waving his fist at the car. "You
villains!" he shouted. "Scoundrels!"
Toad didn't say anything but,
"Poop! Poop!"

Mole went to calm the horse and check the caravan. "It's ruined," he said sadly. "Oh Toad..."

"Who cares about that horrible little cart?" scoffed Toad. "A car is the only way to travel."

And he talked of nothing else, all the way back to Toad Hall.

Chapter 3

The Wild Wood

After their ruined caravan trip,
Mole and Rat stayed quietly by the
river. Many of Rat's friends looked
in for a chat, but never Badger.
Leaves fell and chill winds blew.
Rat stayed inside, snoozing
by the fire.

So, one cold afternoon, Mole slipped out to visit Badger himself. He felt quite cheerful as he entered the Wild Wood... until dusk fell.

The wood, already dark, grew darker. Strange shadows danced about him. Then a whistling began – faint, shrill and all around.

In a panic,
Mole began to
run, bumping into
things and falling
over. Shaking with fear,
he hid in the hollow of an
old oak tree – lost, worn out
and very, very scared.

Meanwhile, Rat had woken up. "Moly!" he called but there was no answer. He saw Mole's coat and boots were gone and went outside.

There, in the mud, were Mole's tracks – leading straight into the Wild Wood.

Horrified, Rat grabbed a stick and set off, calling for his friend the whole time.

At last, he heard a little cry. "Ratty, is it really you?" Mole whimpered, from his hiding place. "It really is," said Rat. "Come on. We must go home."

But it had started to snow. Flakes whirled around them, covering the trees and hiding the path.

Rat shivered. "We may have to stay here after all."

They were looking for shelter, when Mole fell over a door-scraper.

To Mole's surprise, Rat laughed and began to dig in the snow.

"I don't see why you're so happy," grumbled Mole. "I've just scraped my shin."

"Don't you see?" panted Rat. "You've found the entrance to Badger's burrow!"

And Mole had.

"Badger!" yelled Rat, banging on the door. "It's Rat and my friend Mole, lost in the snow."

"Ratty?" said Badger, when he opened the door at last. "What are you doing out there? Come in and get yourselves warm."

He led them to a snug kitchen, found them dry clothes and made supper. Over steaming cocoa and oatcakes, they began to talk.

"Tell me all the news," said Badger. "How's Toad?"

Ratty frowned. "Going from bad to worse. He had another car crash last week."

"He's been taken to the hospital three times," added Mole, "and paid out a fortune in fines."

"He's a hopelessly bad driver," finished Rat, with a yawn. "If he carries on like this, he'll be killed."

"In the spring, we shall take him in hand," said Badger firmly. "But now it's time for bed."

The next morning, after a big breakfast to keep out the cold, and then lunch to keep up their strength, Badger waved them off.

"That's enough adventure for me for a while," thought Mole, as they headed for home.

Chapter 4

Talking to Toad

Early next spring, Badger arrived one morning, just as Mole and Rat were finishing breakfast.

"It's time to take Toad in hand!"
Badger declared. "We must go to
Toad Hall at once."

Up at Toad Hall, a shiny red car
sat on the drive. Toad was at the
front door, adjusting his
driving goggles.

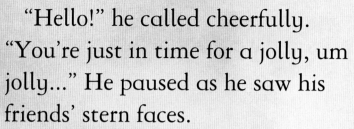

"Hello!" he called cheerfully.
"You're just in time for a jolly, um
jolly..." He paused as he saw his
friends' stern faces.

"Inside," ordered Badger. "We're
going to your study for a talk."

"Talking won't work," muttered
Rat.

Almost an hour later, Badger
and Toad came out of the study.
  "Toad is very sorry for his
foolishness with cars," said Badger.
"Aren't you, Toad?"
      "No!" Toad said. "Not sorry
      at all. In fact, the very next
      car I see, poop-poop! Off I
      shall go."

"Then we shall hide your keys
and lock you in your bedroom until
you see sense," said Badger. "We'll
take turns keeping watch."

Rat was on duty when Toad
asked for a doctor and a lawyer.
"Oh Ratty, I feel so... oh dear,"
Toad moaned faintly.

Rat was alarmed. "Toad must be really ill," he thought, racing from the room and locking the door behind him. "I'd better get help."

Toad laughed as he
watched Rat scurry from
Toad Hall. Swiftly, he
knotted his bedsheets
together, climbed out of
his bedroom window and
slid to the ground.

"I'm just too clever for Ratty!" Toad thought as he briskly walked away. "He's no match for me."

Feeling very pleased with himself, he went on until he reached an inn. Outside, was the most magnificent car Toad had ever seen.

"There's no harm in just *looking* at it," he said to himself. And then, "I wonder if it starts easily?"

As if in a dream, Toad started the engine...

as if in a dream, he climbed into the driver's seat...

and, as if in a dream, he drove off at top speed...

Chapter 5

Toad's adventures

The very next day, he was in court.
"Toad," said the Judge fiercely,
"you stole a valuable car. You
drove it very badly. *And* you were
rude to a policeman. I am sending
you to prison for twenty years!"

"This is the end of everything," Toad sobbed, as he sat in a lonely dungeon. "Oh wise Badger, oh clever Rat, oh sensible Mole. And stupid, stupid Toad."

Toad was too miserable to eat. The jailer's daughter noticed and it made her sad to see him so thin and unhappy.

"Cheer up Toad," she said. "See what I've brought you," and she handed him a plate piled high with hot buttered toast.

Toad dried his eyes, nibbled at the toast and began to feel better.

The jailer's daughter started to visit regularly. As the days went by, she grew to like him.

"Toad," she began, on one visit, "my aunt is a washerwoman..."

"Never mind," said Toad.

"Do be quiet," she said. "My aunt does the prisoners' washing and I think she can help you escape..."

That night, a small, stout figure
hurried from the prison in the dress
and shawl of a washerwoman,
hidden behind a pile
of washing.

"Goodnight ma'am," said a
prison guard.

Toad chuckled to himself.

"'Night!" he squeaked in reply.

46

Toad stumbled through fields,
over ditches and under
hedges, until he was too
tired to go on.

With a huge yawn,
and pulling the shawl
tight around him, he
collapsed by a tree
and slept.

When Toad woke up the next
morning, he wondered where he
was. Then, with a leap of his heart,
he remembered – he was free!
 He stood up, stretched
and marched
out into the
morning sun.

Before long, he reached a canal.
A solitary horse was plodding along
the tow path, pulling a yellow
barge with a smiling bargewoman.

48

Toad barely heard her friendly
greeting.

"Is anything wrong?" she asked.

"Well ma'am," he replied, "I
need to get to Toad Hall to do the,
um, washing and-"

"This is a bit of luck!" the woman interrupted. "I'm going that way now – and I have a pile of washing to be done."

"You are?" said Toad. "Pile of washing..." he added, doubtfully.

"Climb on," she said. "I'll give you a lift and you can do my washing on the way."

Toad stepped aboard with a grin. "I am so clever," he thought.

"Washing's in the cabin," said the bargewoman.

Toad shrugged. "How hard can washing be?" he muttered.

After half an hour of fighting the clothes, Toad was hot and drenched but the clothes were as dirty as ever.

The bargewoman laughed. "You're not a washerwoman at all."

51

"How dare you laugh at me," Toad roared. "I'll have you know I'm a very distinguished Toad."

The bargewoman screamed. "A slimy toad? On my barge? Never!" And, grabbing him by an arm and a leg, she flung him overboard.

Toad went flying through the air and landed with a loud splash in the canal. Gasping for breath, he struggled to the bank, fighting his dress all the way. "It's all over," he wailed. "I shall be caught again."

"What's wrong?" asked a voice. Toad looked up to see a familiar face. A small brown face with whiskers. "Ratty?" he said.

"Toad?" said Rat. "Is that you?
Whatever happened?"

"I've had such trials," boasted
Toad. "Thrown into prison, then
escaped. Come to Toad Hall and
I'll tell you the whole amazing tale."

"Oh Toad, we can't," said Rat.
"The Wild Wooders have
taken it over."

Chapter 6

A surprise attack

A shocked Toad followed Rat home.
"Now don't worry," said Rat,
once Toad had dried off. "Badger
has a plan to recapture Toad Hall."

Just then, Mole and Badger came in. "Ratty, we attack tonight!" said Mole. "They're having a party and Badger knows a secret tunnel that leads right into Toad Hall and..."

He stopped as he saw Toad. "Toad, you're home! Whatever happened?"

"It's quite a story..." Toad began.

"No time for that now," said Badger. "We must prepare."

That night, armed with sticks
and swords, the four of them crept
into the secret tunnel. They groped
and shuffled along, until at last
Badger stopped. "We ought to be
under the Hall now."

As they paused, they heard a
murmur of shouting, cheering and
stomping from above.

57

The tunnel sloped up and they came through a trap door, into the kitchen. Such a noise was coming from the main hall, there was little danger they'd be overheard.

"NOW boys!" shouted Badger
and they ran into the hall.

59

Squealing and screeching filled
the air as terrified weasels dived
through windows and startled
stoats shot under the table.

Badger, Mole and Rat dashed around, bopping anyone who got in their way. As for Toad, he went straight for the Chief Weasel and sent him flying.

In five minutes, it was all over.
"Well done everyone!" said
Badger. "I think we should have
a party of our own to celebrate."

"Dear friends," Toad said, over
a jolly supper. "Thank you for all
your help. I wouldn't have my
home back without you."

And, from that night, Toad was a changed animal. Instead of being boastful or reckless, he was content to live a quiet life by the river with his three best friends.

Kenneth Grahame (1859-1932)

Kenneth Grahame spent part of his childhood with his grandmother, in Cookham Dene, Berkshire, in England. He loved playing in her garden by the river, and exploring the nearby woods.

When he grew up, he worked for the Bank of England, but he wrote in his spare time. *The Wind in the Willows* was written for his son, Alastair, and first published in 1908.

Designed by Hannah Ahmed

First published in 2007 by Usborne Publishing Ltd., Usborne House, 83-85 Saffron Hill, London EC1N 8RT, England. www.usborne.com
Copyright © 2007 Usborne Publishing Ltd.